Hey Diddle Diddle

A Food Chain Tale

by Pam Kapchinske

illustrated by Sherry Rogers

A shiny green beetle was a strollin' along
tappin' his feet and singin' a song.
He said, "Hey diddle diddle—whaddaya know?
I've got six legs to help me go."

A slithering snake came slinkin' past
when he spotted that bug—a snack at last!
He swallowed it whole and shimmied along,
a hissin' and a grinnin' and a singin' a song.

He sang, "Hey diddle diddle—I'm feelin' fine.
Call me cold-blooded, but I've got a spine."
A hawk looked down a tweetin' a tune
and said, "I'd like some breakfast soon."

He snatched that snake right off the ground.
Gobbled him up without a sound
and sang, "Hey diddle diddle—I don't ask why
I've got feathers to help me fly."

He flapped his wings and he was gone
when a frog kerplunked into the pond.
He sang, "Hey, diddle diddle—it's certainly true
the water is nice and the land is too."

A passing bass just shook his head.
"I disagree with you," he said.
"I just like water on my scales.
It fills my gills and wets my tail."

He swallowed that frog—it didn't take long.
Then he slipped away, just a singin' this song:
he sang, "Hey diddle diddle—it can't be wrong,
I love to swim all day long."

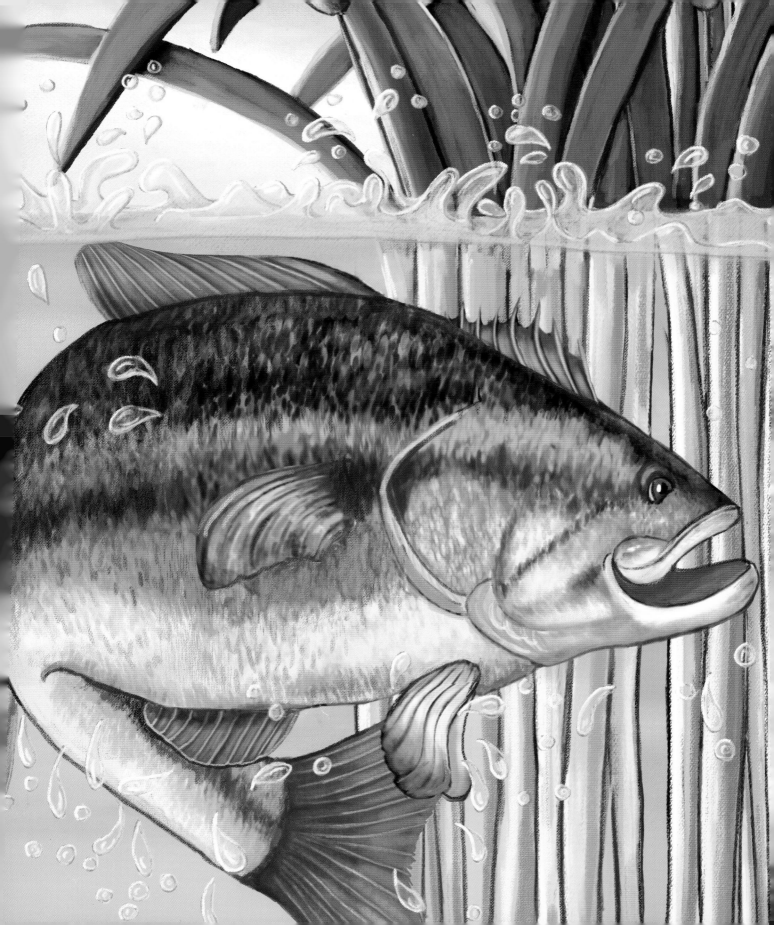

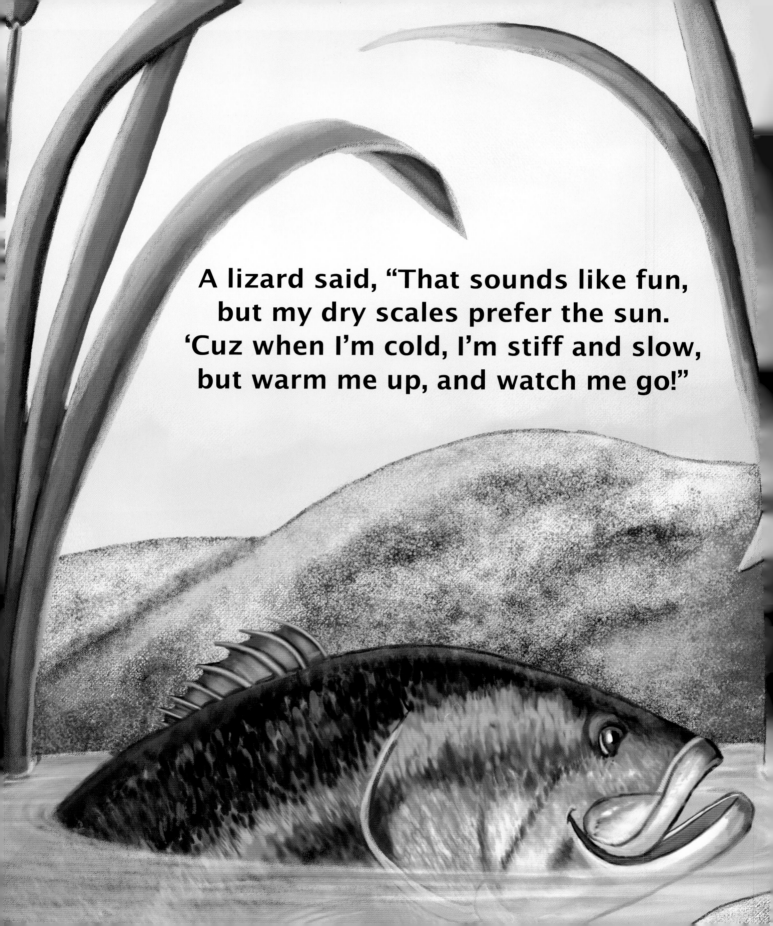

A lizard said, "That sounds like fun, but my dry scales prefer the sun. 'Cuz when I'm cold, I'm stiff and slow, but warm me up, and watch me go!"

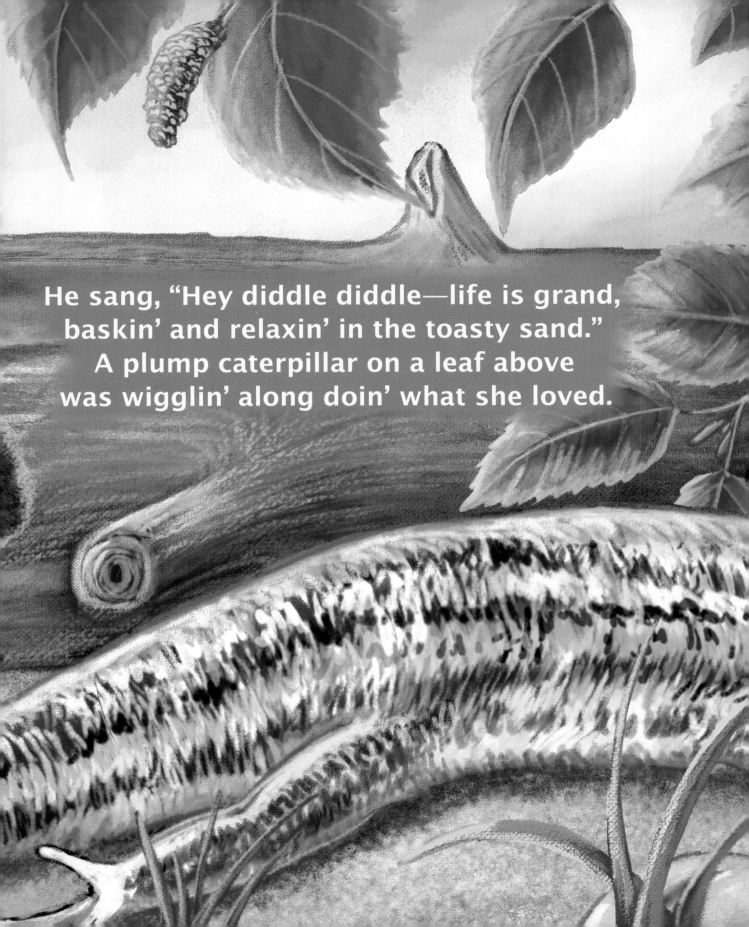

He sang, "Hey diddle diddle—life is grand,
baskin' and relaxin' in the toasty sand."
A plump caterpillar on a leaf above
was wigglin' along doin' what she loved.

She sang, "Hey diddle diddle—it can't be beat:
munchin' and a crunchin' on a leafy treat."
But she nibbled so much, the leaf gave way.
The lizard grinned, "My lucky day!"

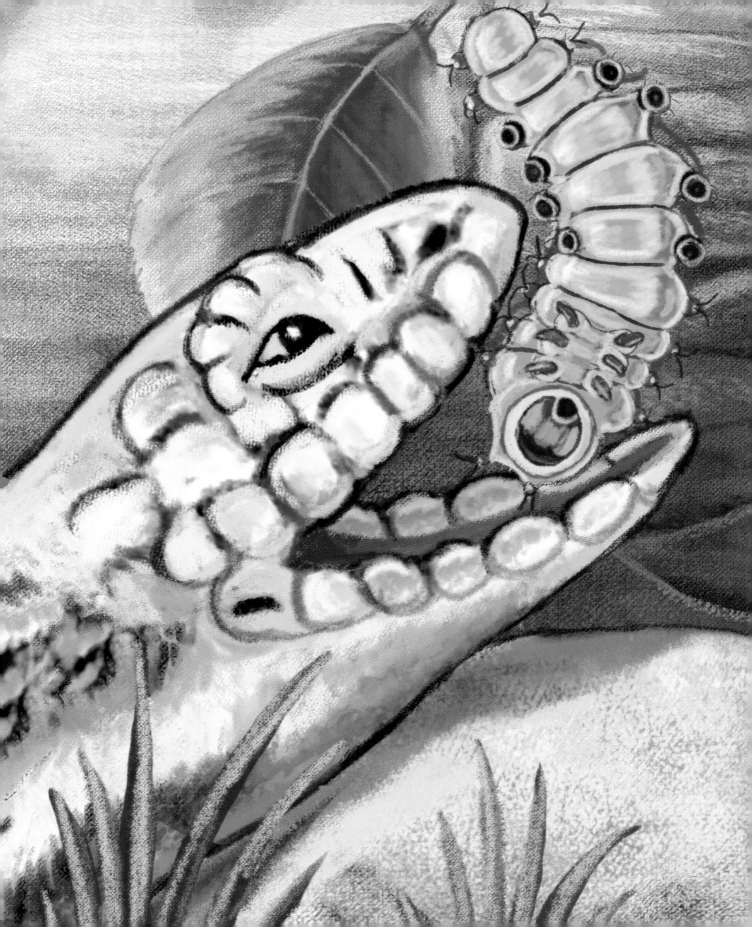

He gulped that snack—a sweet surprise,
said, "Now I'm feelin' energized!"
But a sneaky bobcat, smooth and sly
was crouching in the brush nearby.

And when that lizard dashed away,
the bobcat pounced upon her prey.
She wolfed it down and licked her fur,
aid, "I love fast food," and started to purr.

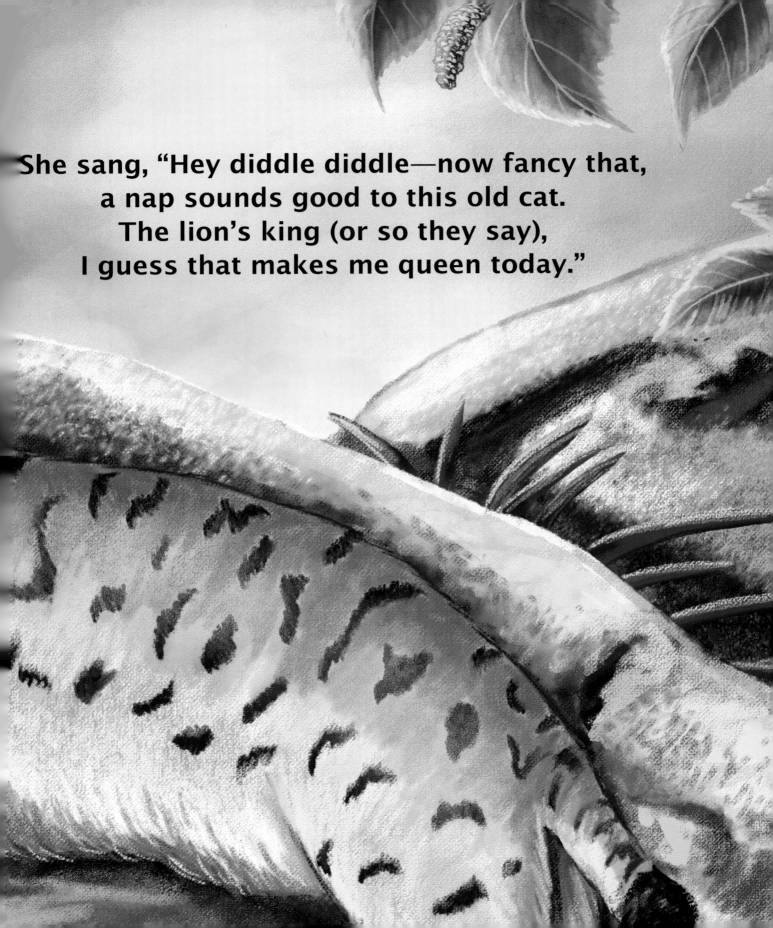

She sang, "Hey diddle diddle—now fancy that,
a nap sounds good to this old cat.
The lion's king (or so they say),
I guess that makes me queen today."

For Creative Minds

Use the information in the story to answer the following questions. Answers are upside dow

Herbivore or Carnivore?

Plants (producers) make their own food from sunlight (photosynthesis). Most plants absorb nutrients from soil using roots. Soil nutrients come from decaying things that were once alive.

   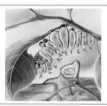

Animals that eat plants are called **consumers** or herbivores. Which animal in the story is an herbivore? What part of a plant was it eating?

Animals that eat other animals are **carnivores**. The bobcat is a carnivore. What animal did it eat?

Predator or Prey?

A carnivore is a **predator** that has to find other animals to eat (prey). A predator of one animal might be prey for another animal. Which is predator and which is prey?

beetle and snake   snake and hawk   bass and frog

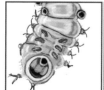    

caterpillar and lizard   lizard and bobcat

Food Chains: True or False?

...l of the plants and animals that are eaten by or that eat a particular animal are ...art of that animal's food chain. A habitat will have many different food chains that are ...nked together, called a food web. The plants and animals in this book all live in or ...round freshwater. Using the information in the book, see if you can figure out which ...atements are true and which are false.

1 The hawk, fish, and bobcat are shown in the same food chain.

2 A healthy adult animal is at the top of its food chain if it does not have natural predators. The snake is at the top of its food chain.

3 Nothing eats animals that are at the top of their food chain.

4 Habitats are communities of plants, animals, and non-living things that interact in certain locations. In order for plants and animals to be in the same food chain, they must be in the same habitat.

Animal Classification

Use the information in the story to identify the animal. Then use the clue(s) and the animal classification information to figure out to which animal class the animal belongs. Answers are upside down, below.

Vertebrates are animals that have backbones.
Invertebrates do not have backbones.

Warm-blooded animals make their own hea
and have a constant body temperature.
Cold-blooded animals' body temperature comes from their surroundings.

Reptiles (vertebrates) have dry scales or plates, are cold-blooded, use lungs to breathe oxygen from the air, and most young hatch from eggs.	Mammals (vertebrates) have hair, fur, or whiskers; are warm-blooded; use lungs to breathe oxygen from the air; and most are born alive.
Birds (vertebrates) are the only animals with feathers, are warm-blooded, use lungs to breathe oxygen from the air, and all young hatch from eggs.	Amphibians (vertebrates) have soft, moist skin and are cold-blooded. Most young (tadpoles or larvae) live in water and use gills to breathe; adults live on land and use lungs to breathe.
Most fishes (vertebrates) have wet, slime-covered scales. All fishes are cold-blooded, use gills to breathe, and can either be born alive or hatch from eggs.	Insects (invertebrates) have hard outer covering. Adults have three body parts: head, thorax, & abdomen; three pairs of (six) legs, usually two pairs of wings and one pair of antennae. Most hatch from eggs but some have live birth.

1. Which animal has six legs?
2. Which animal is cold-blooded and has a spine (another word for backbone)?
3. Which animal has feathers to help it fly?
4. Which animal likes land and water?
5. Which animal has gills and wet scales?
6. Which animal has dry scales?
7. Which animal has fur?

Answers: 1) beetle/insect, 2) snake/reptile and bass/fish, 3) hawk/bird, 4) frog/amphibian, 5) bass/fish, 6) lizard/reptile, 7) bobcat/mammal

Animal Adaptations Matching

n you match the animal to its description? Answers are upside down.

 snake

 beetle

 frog

 hawk

 bass

 bobcat

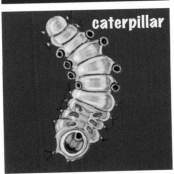 caterpillar

 lizard

1 I'm a young insect. When I grow up, I'll be a moth or a butterfly.

2 My back feet have webs to help me swim through the water.

3 I don't have any legs so I slither on the ground. I use my forked tongue to sense what's around me.

4 I use my tail to push me through the water.

5 I use my sharp teeth and claws to catch my prey.

6 I shed my skin when I grow and use my tongue to help smell what's around me, just like a snake.

7 I don't have bones but I do have a hard outer shell to protect me.

8 I use my sharp talons to grab prey and to hold onto tree branches.

Answers: 1) caterpillar, 2) frog, 3) snake, 4) bass, 5) bobcat, 6) lizard, 7) beetle, 8) hawk

To my sons, Noah and Kai—PK

To my wonderful Father, who always kept me safe and secure. I will cherish his memory always—SR

The author is donating a portion of her royalties to support the efforts of Project Wildlife of San Diego Coun

Thanks to Loran Wlodarski, Science Writer at SeaWorld Orlando, for verifying the accuracy of the informatior this book.

Library of Congress Cataloging-in-Publication Data

Kapchinske, Pam, 1971-
   Hey diddle diddle : a food chain tale / by Pam Kapchinske ; illustrated by Sherry Rogers.
      p. cm.
   ISBN 978-1-60718-130-9 (hardcover) -- ISBN 978-1-60718-140-8 (softcover) -- ISBN 978-1-60718-150-7
(english ebook) -- ISBN 978-1-60718-160-6 (spanish ebook) 1. Food chains (Ecology)--Juvenile literature. 2.
Pond animals--Juvenile literature. 3. Pond ecology--Juvenile literature. 4. Riparian animals--Juvenile literatur
5. Riparian ecology--Juvenile literature. I. Rogers, Sherry, ill. II. Title.
   QH541.14.K37 2011
   577'.16--dc23
                              2011016336

Also available as eBooks featuring auto-flip, auto-read, 3D-page-curling, and
selectable English and Spanish text and audio
Interest level: 003-008
Grade level: P-3
Lexile Level: 820 Lexile Code: AD
Curriculum keywords: adaptations, anthropomorphic, food web, life science:
general, prediction, repeated lines, repeating earth patterns, rhythm or rhyme,
classification, producer/carnivore/herbivore, predator/prey

Manufactured in China, June, 2011
This product conforms to CPSIA 2008
First Printing
Published by Sylvan Dell Publishing
Mt. Pleasant, SC 29464